Happy Birthday, Hedgehog!

ACORN™
SCHOLASTIC INC.

Norm Feuti

To Katie, Maria, and Brian —NF

Library of Congress Cataloging-in-Publication Data

Names: Feuti, Norman, author, illustrator.
Title: Happy birthday, Hedgehog! / Norm Feuti.
Description: First edition. | New York : Acorn/Scholastic Inc., 2022. |
Series: Hello, Hedgehog! ; 6 | Audience: Ages 4–6. | Audience: Grades K–1. |
Summary: Harry is worried when he discovers someone has given his
best friend, Hedgehog, the exact same birthday gift he brought, but Hedgehog
reassures his best pal that since he now has two airplanes, he can race them with Harry.
Identifiers: LCCN 2021033712 (print) |
ISBN 9781338677188 (library binding) | ISBN 9781338677171 (paperback) |
Subjects: CYAC: Birthdays—Fiction. | Parties—Fiction. |
Hedgehogs—Fiction. | Best friends—Fiction. | Friendship—Fiction.
Classification: LCC PZ7.1.F52 Hap 2022 (print) |
DDC [E]—dc23

LC record available at https://lccn.loc.gov/2021033712

10 9 8 7 6 5 4 3 2 1   22 23 24 25 26

Printed in China   62
First edition, May 2022
Edited by Katie Carella
Book design by Maria Mercado

2

3

6

Tick.
Tick.
Tick.

I know!

WIND-UP PLANE

9

Snip.
Snip.

CRAYONS

WIND-UP PL

CRAYONS

Ta-da!

Tick.
Tick.
Tick.

I am also very late!

Tink!

I will open this one first.

It is from my friend Luna.

It is a puzzle! Yay!
I love puzzles!

Rip!

25

I will have to write Otter a nice letter!

Harry? Are you oka

Um . . . no.

What is wrong?

28

Whizz! **Whizz!**

You won, Hedgehog!

Yay! Let's go again!

Whizz!

Norm Feuti lives in Massachusetts with his family, a dog, two cats, and a guinea pig. He is the creator of the newspaper comic strips **Retail** and **Gil**. He is also the author and illustrator of the graphic novel series **Beak and Ally**. **Hello, Hedgehog!** is Norm's first early reader series.

1. Draw a jelly bean shape.

2. Add the eyes, ears, nose, and mouth.

3. Draw a triangle hat, and a box shape.

4. Give Hedgehog arms, legs and lots of quills. Put black spots on the ends of the quills.

5. Draw the eyebrows, a big smile, and put a bow on the present.

6. Color in your drawing!

WHAT'S YOUR STORY?

It is Hedgehog's birthday! Harry gives him a present.
Imagine **you** go to Hedgehog's birthday party.
What present would you bring? Would you wrap it?
What party games would you play?
Write and draw your story!